MICHAEL
JORDAN

BY RICHARD RAMBECK

*(Photo on
front cover)*

*Michael Jordan goes
after a loose ball in a
game against the
Detroit Pistons.*

*(Photo on
previous pages)*

*Michael Jordan fakes a
move against Utah
Jazz's Jeff Hornacek in
Chicago, Illinois.
January 25, 1998*

GRAPHIC DESIGN
Robert A. Honey, Seattle

PHOTO RESEARCH
James R. Rothaus, James R. Rothaus & Associates

**ELECTRONIC PRE-PRESS
PRODUCTION**
Robert E. Bonaker, Graphic Design & Consulting Co.

PHOTOGRAPHY
All photos Associated Press AP

Library of Congress Cataloging-in-Publication Data
Rambeck, Richard
Michael Jordan / by Richard Rambeck
p. cm.
Summary: Examines the life of the star player for the
Chicago Bulls and describes his accomplishments
within the National Basketball Association.
ISBN 1-56766-520-9 (library : reinforced : alk. paper)

1. Jordan, Michael, 1963- — Juvenile literature.
2. Basketball players—United States—Biography—Juvenile
literature.
[1. Jordan, Michael, 1963- . 2. Basketball players. 3. Afro-
Americans—Biography.] I. Title
GV884.J67R36 1998   97-44096
796.323'092 — dc21   CIP
[B]   AC

CONTENTS

Jordan slam dunks the ball in a game against the Utah Jazz at Salt Lake City.

Was it all slipping away for the Chicago Bulls? They seemed to be in control of the 1997 National Basketball Association final series. They had beaten the Utah Jazz in the first two games, both of which were played in Chicago. When the series moved to Utah for the next three games, the Bulls weren't themselves. They lost two in a row. The experts, who hadn't given the Jazz a chance when the series started, now wondered if the Bulls were too old to be champs again. Even the great Michael Jordan seemed to be slipping.

GAME FIVE

The morning of game five, Jordan woke up with the stomach flu. Hours before the most important game of the season, he wasn't sure whether he could even play. "I've played many seasons with Michael," said forward Scottie Pippen, "and I've never seen him as sick. It was to the point where I didn't think he was

7

going to put his uniform on." Jordan did put on his uniform, but he wasn't his usual self. He was tired, and he was weak. "I knew I had to play in spurts, with bursts of energy and then rest for a few minutes," Jordan said.

JORDAN'S WILL TO WIN

It was Utah that had the burst of energy at the beginning of the game. Led by their stars, forward Karl Malone and guard John Stockton, the Jazz raced to a 16–point lead in the first quarter. Utah, in fact, led for most of the game, but the Jazz couldn't shake the Bulls. Jordan wasn't at his best, but he was keeping Chicago in the game. "In the third quarter, I felt like I was going to pass out," Jordan said. "I felt like I couldn't really catch my wind. In the fourth quarter, I don't know how I got through it."

Jordan shooting a basket against the Utah Jazz, January 25, 1998. Scottie Pippen watches as Jeff Hornacek is unable to check the shot.

COME FROM BEHIND

Jordan not only got through the quarter, he led the Bulls from behind. Chicago trailed 77–69 with 10 minutes left in the game. Jordan then scored three baskets, including a three–pointer. Forward Toni Kukoc added another three–pointer to give the Bulls a 79–77 lead. In the last minute, Chicago was behind 85–84. Jordan was fouled and went to the line. He had already scored 11 points in the quarter. He made the first foul shot to tie the game. He then missed the second, but the Bulls got the rebound.

SWEET VICTORY

Jordan had the ball in his hands again. With 25 seconds left, he jumped in the air and fired a three–pointer. "It was there," Jordan said of the shot. "I had just missed one the time before. I certainly didn't want to go into overtime." The ball went straight into the basket, giving Chicago an 88–85 lead. The Bulls won 90–88 to take a three games to two lead in the series. Jordan topped all scorers with 38 points, including 15 in the fourth quarter. He simply refused to let the Bulls lose, even though he probably should have been in bed.

BACK TO CHICAGO

"The effort that he came out and gave us was just incredible," Pippen said. "He just kept making big shot after big shot." Jordan's performance in game five turned the series around. The Bulls went back to Chicago knowing they needed only one victory to wrap up their fifth championship in seven years. Utah gave the Bulls a real battle in game six, but Jordan was just too good. He scored 39 points and grabbed 11 rebounds, leading Chicago to a 90–86 victory. Jordan was voted the Most Valuable Player of the NBA final series for the fifth time.

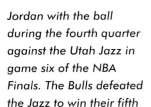

Jordan with the ball during the fourth quarter against the Utah Jazz in game six of the NBA Finals. The Bulls defeated the Jazz to win their fifth NBA championship.

Jordan smiles after winning another trophy, the MVP award for the 1996 NBA All Star game, February 11, 1996. He scored 20 points as the East won 129–118.

"GREATEST PLAYER"

"He's the greatest player I've ever seen play," said Utah coach Jerry Sloan. Pippen agreed. "No matter what's out there, what there is for him to overcome, he's been able to overcome it. . . . No matter how you look at it, he's the greatest player ever to play this game. And he proves it night in and night out." No NBA player has scored as many points per game as Jordan has. His 31.7 scoring average is the highest in league history. He also has nine NBA scoring titles, two more than anybody else does.

LEAVING THE GAME

Michael Jordan nearly left the game of basketball for good after the 1992–93 season. He led the Bulls to their third straight NBA title. He averaged 41 points per game in the finals against the Phoenix Suns. Chicago won the series in six games, and Jordan was voted the MVP of the finals. Everyone expected him to return for the 1993–94 season and

15

try to carry the Bulls to a fourth straight championship. Jordan, however, felt he had nothing left to prove on the basketball court. He had won three NBA titles and been voted league MVP three times as well.

Jordan sails high knocking away a shot during the Summer Olympics in Barcelona, Spain, July 27, 1992. This was the second time he was to play in the Olympic games.

A NEW CHALLENGE

Jordan had also won two Olympic gold medals in basketball and played on an NCAA championship team at the University of North Carolina. He still loved the game, but he wanted a new challenge. A few weeks before the start of the 1993–94 season, Jordan decided to retire from the Bulls. He said he wanted to try a new sport, one he hadn't played since high school — baseball! Many baseball scouts said Jordan was crazy if he thought he could ever reach the major leagues. They said he was a low–level minor league player at best.

Jordan set out to prove the baseball experts wrong. After the Chicago White Sox signed him to a minor league contract, Jordan worked hard to improve. He played the 1994 season for the Birmingham Barons, Chicago's AA minor league team. An outfielder, Jordan batted .202 with three home runs and 51 RBIs. He also stole 30 bases. Jordan planned to play baseball again in 1995, but something changed his mind. That something was how much he still loved playing basketball. "I just decided that I love the game too much to stay away," he said.

JORDAN RETURNS

Jordan returned to the Bulls late in the 1994–95 season. He averaged 26.9 points a game during the regular season and 31.5 points in the playoffs. Chicago, however, lost in the Eastern Conference semifinals to the Orlando Magic. That marked the second straight year the Bulls had failed to win the league title. The 1995–96 season would be a different story, though, because Jordan played a

19

full season for the first time in three years. And what a full season it was. Chicago won 72 out of 82 games during the regular season. It was the most victories ever by a NBA team in one year.

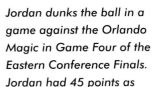

FOUR TIME MVP

Jordan won his eighth scoring title and was voted regular season MVP for the fourth time. In the playoffs, the Bulls continued their winning ways. They swept Miami in three games in the first round, beat the New York Knicks four games to one in the second round, and swept Orlando in four straight in the Eastern Conference finals. In the league finals, Chicago defeated the Western Conference champion Seattle Sonics in six games. Jordan, who averaged 27.3 points per game in the finals, was voted MVP.

Jordan hustles downcourt to play defense during a game against the Philadelphia 76ers. Jordan finished with 18 points in 24 minutes as the Bulls defeated the Sixers 113–101. October 24, 1997.

"SUPERMAN"

How good is Michael Jordan? He is, quite simply, the best who has ever played the game. Many experts believe that if he hadn't retired to play baseball, he would have led the Bulls to seven straight NBA titles going into the 1997–98 season. "Michael might be the closest thing to Superman," said Philadelphia coach Larry Brown. Former NBA guard Kenny Smith said Jordan could make Yakima (a minor league team in the Continental Basketball Association) a contender for the NBA championship. "The man is that good," Smith said.